Thanks to Marylin Hafner for her ingenious contribution to Santa's world.
M.W.S.

For Abigail and Douglas, Jennifer and Amanda…future Santas.
M.H.

Text copyright © 1990 by Marjorie Weinman Sharmat
Illustrations copyright © 1990 by Marylin Hafner
ALL RIGHTS RESERVED
Printed in the United States of America
FIRST EDITION
Library of Congress Cataloging-in-Publication Data

Sharmat, Marjorie Weinman.
I'm Santa Claus and I'm famous / Marjorie Weinman Sharmat ;
illustrated in full color by Marylin Hafner.
p.   cm.
Summary: On Career Day Santa Claus visits school
and tells the children how he was trained
for his job by the old Santa.
ISBN 0-8234-0826-4
1. Santa Claus—Juvenile fiction.   [1. Santa Claus—Fiction.]
I. Hafner, Marylin, ill.   II. Title.
PZ7.S5299Imp   1990
[E]—dc20   90-55106   CIP   AC
ISBN 0-8234-0826-4

I'M SANTA CLAUS
and
I'M FAMOUS

by Marjorie Weinman Sharmat

illustrated by
Marylin Hafner

Holiday House/New York

091082

I wasn't always famous.

When I was little, my parents had BIG plans for me.

I ASKED MY FRIENDS WHAT THEY WERE GOING TO BE WHEN THEY GREW UP.

Jennie was going to be a veterinarian.

Peter was going to be a painter.

Mona was going to be a farmer.

I was the **ONLY ONE** who was going

to be SANTA CLAUS. My training began...

WHEN I WAS SIX, I GOT A SLEIGH FOR MY BIRTHDAY.

HOPE YOU LIKE IT, SON.

THIS WILL BE MORE FUN THAN A BICYCLE!

Happy Birthday Mom & Dad

WHEN I WAS EIGHT... EIGHT(8)

GOLLY GEE WILLIKINS!

FOR OUR BOY

REINDEER ARRIVED...

THEN there was the day my parents brought the elves home for me to meet.

They were very small and very busy.

I was busy, too.
I had to read all the letters the mailman brought.

IT'LL BE GOOD TRAINING FOR THE SACKS AND SACKS OF MAIL YOU'LL GET WHEN YOU'RE SANTA.

READ THESE MAPS TOO. YOU'LL HAVE TO KNOW YOUR WAY AROUND THE ENTIRE WORLD WHEN YOU'RE SANTA.

THE ENTIRE WORLD! THIS IS GETTING BETTER AND BETTER!

WHAT IS THE CAPITAL OF IOWA?

NEXT came my sports training. While my friends were busy playing football and hockey, I had my own sport. I climbed down chimneys. Down and up, up and down.

I became the STAR of the school cafeteria.

TIME PASSED...

Then on a certain December 24th, when I was practicing going down and up and up and down the chimney,

I heard a *WHOOSH!* It was Santa.

Then Santa reached down and scooped me up. Before I knew it, we were climbing up the chimney and into his sleigh.

ALLEY-OOP!

WE'RE OFF TO EUROPE!

WHERE ARE WE GOING?

EUROPE? DOES THAT MEAN WE'RE LEAVING MY NEIGHBORHOOD?

THE WHOLE WORLD WILL BE YOUR NEIGHBORHOOD. NOW PAY ATTENTION...

I learned how to leave presents. You don't just *dump* them off.

Switzerland has the most interesting rooftops.

Russia takes a long time.

The reindeer love to loop over England.

I LOVED IT! All those special people all over the world getting presents from Santa.

Santa came back year…

after

year

after

year.

AND THEN...

Last DECEMBER 24th, Santa Claus came around and handed me a huge sack of presents....